Bookclub-in-a-Box presents the discussion companion for Jeffrey Eugenides' novel

Middlesex

Published by Alfred A. Knopf Canada and Farrar, Straus and Giroux (U.S.A.) 2002. ISBN: 0-676-97564-X

Quotations used in this guide have been taken from the text of the hardcover edition of **Middlesex**. All information taken from other sources is acknowledged.

This discussion companion for **Middlesex** has been prepared and written by Marilyn Herbert, originator of Bookclub-in-a-Box. Marilyn Herbert. B.Ed., is a teacher, librarian, speaker and writer. Bookclub-in-a-Box is a unique guide to current fiction and classic literature intended for book club discussions, educational study seminars, and personal pleasure. For more information about the Bookclub-in-a-Box team, visit our website.

Bookclub-in-a-Box discussion companion for Middlesex

ISBN 10: 1-897082-00-2
ISBN 13: 978-1897082-00-3

This guide reflects the perspective of the Bookclub-in-a-Box team and is the sole property of Bookclub-in-a-Box.

©2005 BOOKCLUB-IN-A-BOX
©2007 2ND EDITION SE

Unauthorized reproduction of this book or its contents for republication in whole or in part is strictly prohibited.

CONTACT INFORMATION: SEE BACK COVER.

BOOKCLUB-IN-A-BOX
Jeffrey Eugenides' Middlesex

READERS AND LEADERS GUIDE . 2

INTRODUCTION

Suggested Beginnings 7

Novel Quickline 8

Key to the Novel 10

Author Information 11

CHARACTERIZATION

Mythmakers 18

Nymphs 24

The Chorus 26

FOCUS POINTS / THEMES

Transformation, Identity . . .33

Fate and Destiny 35

Creation, Original Sin 36

Duality 37

Punishment and Crime 39

Time 40

Writing Process 41

WRITING STRUCTURE

The Greek Card 47

Greek Gifts 48

The History Card 49

Parallel Suits 50

WRITING STYLE

Layers 56

Language 57

Literary Reference 57

Narrative Voice 58

Humor 60

Observation, Home Movies .61

SYMBOLS

Silk 65

Chekhov's Gun 65

Zora's Diary 66

Hermaphroditus 66

Water and the Bridge 67

Minotaur and the Maze . . .68

Gambling, Numbers 69

BACKGROUND INFORMATION

Hermaphrodism 73

The Myth of Tiresias 74

W.D. Fard 75

Grandpa's Song 77

Carl Jung 78

FROM THE NOVEL (QUOTES) . .81

ACKNOWLEDGEMENTS 89

BOOKCLUB-IN-A-BOX
Readers and Leaders Guide

Each Bookclub-in-a-Box guide is clearly and effectively organized to give you information and ideas for a lively discussion, as well as to present the major highlights of the novel. The format, with a Table of Contents, allows you to pick and choose the specific points you wish to talk about. It does not have to be used in any prescribed order. In fact, it is meant to support, not determine, your discussion.

You Choose What to Use.

You may find that some information is repeated in more than one section and may be cross-referenced so as to provide insight on the same idea from different angles.

The guide is formatted to give you extra space to make your own notes.

How to Begin
Relax and look forward to enjoying your bookclub.

With Bookclub-in-a-Box as your behind the scenes support, there is little for you to do in the way of preparation.

Some readers like to review the guide after reading the novel; some before. Either way, the guide is all you will need as a companion for your discussion. You may find that the guide's interpretation, information, and background have sparked other ideas not included.

Having read the novel and armed with Bookclub-in-a-Box, you will be well prepared to lead or guide or listen to the discussion at hand.

Lastly, if you need some more 'hands-on' support, feel free to contact us. (See Contact Information)

What to Look For

Each Bookclub-in-a-Box guide is divided into easy-to-use sections, which include points on characters, themes, writing style and structure, literary or historical background, author information, and other pertinent features unique to the novel being discussed. These may vary slightly from guide to guide.

INTERPRETATION OF EACH NOVEL REFLECTS THE PERSPECTIVE OF THE BOOKCLUB-IN-A-BOX TEAM.

Do We Need to Agree?
THE ANSWER TO THIS QUESTION IS NO.

If we have sparked a discussion or a debate on certain points, then we are happy. We invite you to share your group's alternative findings and experiences with us. You can respond on-line at our website or contact us through our Contact Information. We would love to hear from you.

Discussion Starters

There are as many ways to begin a bookclub discussion as there are members in your group. If you are an experienced group, you will already have your favorite ways to begin. If you are a newly formed group or a group looking for new ideas, here are some suggestions.

Ask for people's impressions of the novel. (This will give you some idea about which parts of the unit to focus on.)

- Identify a favorite or major character.
- Identify a favorite or major idea.
- Begin with a powerful or pertinent quote. (not necessarily from the novel)
- Discuss the historical information of the novel. (not applicable to all novels)
- If this author is familiar to the group, discuss the range of his/her work and where this novel stands in that range.
- Use the discussion topics and questions in the Bookclub-in-a-Box guide.

If you have further suggestions for discussion starters, be sure to share them with us and we will share them with others.

Above All, Enjoy Yourselves

INTRODUCTION

Suggested Beginnings

Novel Quickline

Key to the Novel

Author Information

INTRODUCTION

Suggested Beginnings

1. Eugenides' goal was to write about the normal process of transformation – puberty and self-discovery – that every human being goes through. To do so, he chose the subject of hermaphrodism, a condition that is not treated as a norm of society, although it has existed since mythical times. He has stated that he wants to make the bizarre normal, rather than portray reality as bizarre.

What are your thoughts about this choice of subject matter? Has Eugenides succeeded?

2. A common criticism of **Middlesex** has been its portrayal of Cal's personality. For many critics, Cal didn't work – too bland, no personality, too noncommittal.

Do you agree? How does Cal/Callie compare with the portrayal of the other characters in the novel? And why do you think Eugenides did this?

3. The opening lines to **Middlesex** may remind readers of the opening paragraph of Charles Dickens' novel, **David Copperfield**: *"To begin my life with the beginning of my life, I record that I was born ... on a Friday, at twelve o'clock at night."* Callie tells us that she *"... was born twice: ... first as a baby girl ... in January of 1960; and then again, as a teenage boy ... in August of 1974."* It is a classic statement that will be remembered because we are immediately engaged.

Compare Callie's opening words to the first lines of any number of other famous classics that you have enjoyed. What makes them memorable?

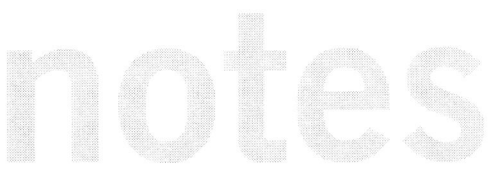

More Questions

There are so many wonderful scenes in this novel.
Which is your favorite? Is it possible to pick only one?
Why do Greek myths and legends still hold a powerful sway over us today?

Considering the fact that Callie is biased in the telling of her own story, is she a reliable narrator? Why does Cal/Callie portray herself so mildly?

With the exception of Cal and Julie, the other characters are vibrant and dramatically interesting.
Who is your favorite? Who is not?

Considering Cal's comment on p.478 about free will making a comeback, discuss the nature vs. nurture debate.
Has it been put to rest? Can it be put to rest?

Novel Quickline

Callie is born a hermaphrodite into a family of Greek immigrants. To understand Callie's journey, she takes us back a couple of generations to the beginning of her story, which starts with Desdemona and Lefty in Bithynios, Turkey. She follows them across the ocean, sees how they re-establish themselves in Detroit together with their children, Milton and Zoë, and how they intersect with Jimmy, Sourmelina, Father Mike, Tessie, and others. From the union of two families comes Callie.

Because Eugenides believes that everything in life and history is connected, he weaves together the story of immigration and birth. Immigrants are a combination of the old and the new, and therefore they can be viewed as hybrids. The offspring of two parents are rarely all one or the other, and they too can be considered hybrids. In fact, nature is full of hybrids and all are perfectly normal.

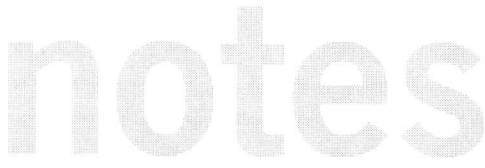

Callie is a hybrid with a small difference. As a hermaphrodite, Callie is a unique combination of man and woman. She was born with two sets of genitalia – one male and the other female – but until she was fourteen, no one, including Callie, knew this. When she does find out, Callie's life takes an abrupt turn. Callie struggles to understand why she, a girl who is not homosexual, is attracted so strongly to other women. She must come to terms with her distinctive place in the universe. She has to learn about who and what she is. And so must the reader.

Eugenides takes a gamble and shows how the roll of genetic dice can create a person like Callie. He uses ancient Greek drama, myth, and legend to explain a biological phenomenon that may sound new but has always existed. He uses the ancient Greek formula – the combination of tragedy and comedy – to characterize and illuminate what being a hermaphrodite is all about.

As a writer, Eugenides knows that a novel is not always just a good read. Like all books, fiction can have another function: to inform the reader of something new and, if applicable, to start a conversation. Hermaphrodism has existed since the beginning of human history, but it has not been the center of mainstream discussions.

Jeffrey Eugenides could have left this topic to the non-fiction writers and to the diarists, but he felt he could use a gripping story and wonderful characters to enlighten his readers in an engaging way. The result is **Middlesex**.

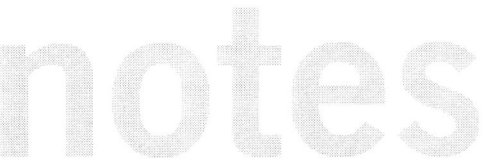

Key to the Novel

Definition and Redefinition

Here are two passages that unlock the story's treasures:

> *Normality wasn't normal. It couldn't be. If normality were normal, everybody could leave it alone.* (p.446)

This idea is central to the novel and its premise: what is the definition of normal? If there is no definition, why do we expend so much energy and effort trying to establish, challenge, defend, and boost normalcy? If there is not an established definition that we seek to follow, then everything should be acceptable.

Blends are normal; hybrids are normal. Nature is filled with cross-pollination and new species. Callie is just a new species.

Definition and redefinition is at the heart of everyone's personality and persona. Everyone is changed or changing: Desdemona, Lefty, Jimmy, and Cal. Even Chapter 11 undergoes the usual sixties university/rock group/drug culture/ political activist/ earth-loving transformation, although he never quite recovers from the change:

> *[the house on Middlesex Avenue is a] ...beacon ... a place designed for a new type of human being, who would inhabit a new world.* (p.529)

The architecture of a house is the same as the formation of the body. Both contain an essence, the soul of those who live within. As a symbol, this house represents all that is right, wrong, and different about Cal or anyone for that matter. The house is atypical in its neighborhood, just as Callie is atypical as a human being. But exceptions are usually found everywhere, and Cal is no exception.

Author Information

There are many biographical details from Eugenides' life that are included in the novel as a frame or a web from which he constructs and spins his story.

Eugenides was born in Grosse Point Park, Michigan, in 1960. (Cal is born in 1960 and moves to Grosse Point after the loss of the restaurant.) He grew up in Detroit and loves the city so much that he has used it as a setting in both of his novels. Eugenides is to Detroit what Philip Roth and Saul Bellow are to New York and the eastern seaboard. The house Eugenides grew up in was located on Middlesex Boulevard. This is just one reason he felt he was destined to write this book and name it **Middlesex**.

Eugenides' father, Constantine, was the son of Greek immigrants (Milton is the son of Greek immigrants) and his mother, Wanda, is of Anglo-Irish heritage. Both his parents were born in Detroit and grew up in Grosse Point. His father does not speak Greek, nor is he overly attached to his Greek heritage. His grandparents, who were silk farmers in the old country, emigrated to Detroit early in the century (like Desdemona). Since Eugenides didn't know his grandparents, he recreated them in his imagination as he would have liked them to be. In addition, he used many of the actual location names that came from his family's history.

As a teen he considered himself a bit of a geek. He always wanted to be a writer and modeled himself after Stephen Dedalus, the main character in Joyce's **A Portrait of the Artist as a Young Man**. He studied English at Brown University and pursued a Master's in English and Creative Writing at Stanford.

His wife, Julie, is a photographer, and they have one daughter. He currently lives in Berlin, a place to which he originally went on a fellowship.

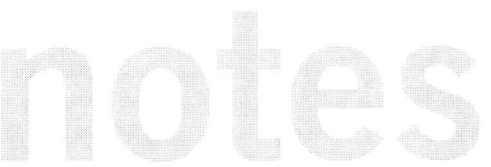

Granta, a literary magazine, published a list in 1996 called "The Twenty Under Forty." This list included the names of America's best young novelists. Eugenides was named on that list, which is now published annually.

His first novel, **The Virgin Suicides** (1991), won the Aga Khan Prize for fiction; and the Writers Award, Whiting foundation, 1993. It also won an Academy of Motion Picture Arts & Sciences fellowship; and a Guggenheim fellowship, 1994. It was adapted into a film by director Sophia Coppola in 2000.

Middlesex, his second novel, took nine years to write. (This is an interesting but unintentional variation on the theme of gestation and birth.) It won the Pulitzer Prize for fiction in 2003, and it was the National Book Critics Circle Award Finalist in 2002. (The winner was Ian McEwan's **Atonement**.)

In his admittedly checkered career, Eugenides has been a cab driver, a busboy, and a volunteer (1982) with Mother Teresa in India; he has been a writer and photographer for *Yachtsman* magazine, and a newsletter editor for the American Academy of Poets. He occasionally writes pop-music essays.

Inspiration for this Novel

- After reading Michel Foucault's **The History of Sexuality**, Eugenides came across the memoir of a real hermaphrodite, Herculine Barbin, who lived in the nineteenth century. He was intrigued by her story and thought of it as a medical mystery, a story of *"personal transformation and doomed passion."* (Gale)

- His interest turned to research, and he came across the 5-alpha-reductase deficiency syndrome, which originates in small, isolated, and inbred communities, similar to the place from where his grandparents came. He wanted to discuss the subject of hermaphrodism, and he now saw an opportunity to recreate his family history within an epic tale.

- Like other writers of the post-modern, post-war era, Eugenides is fascinated by the writing process and how it connects to the reader and the reader's life. He sees the novelist as having a hermaphroditic imagination, because the narrator/writer has to reach into the thoughts and motivations of both men and women. Eugenides does just that in the character of Cal/Callie.

- **Middlesex** is also the vehicle for the social and cultural commentary that Eugenides wants to make. It is an immigration story, the story of the beginning of industrialization in the U.S., and it includes the beginnings of the Black Muslim movement. It is a time capsule of a half century of American life.

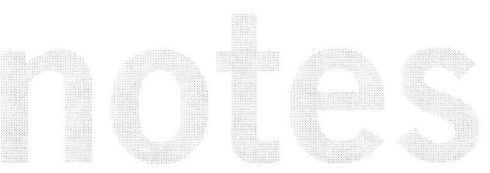

CHARACTERIZATION

Mythmakers

Nymphs

The Chorus

CHARACTERIZATION

All of the characters in the book are wonderfully expressive, with the exception of the adult Cal and his girlfriend, Julie, who seem subdued and mild. Possible explanations for this might include the following:

- Eugenides did not wish to take anything away from the charm and innocence of the child, Callie.

- Callie as an observer tries to maintain an air of the dispassionate narrator who is careful not to taint the narration with an impassioned bias.

- The novel attempts to highlight the fact that what society considers "abnormal" is merely dull and unsensational.

As in every good Greek drama, there is a cast of thousands. For the purposes of this guide, they are divided up according to the roles they play: mythmakers, nymphs, chorus.

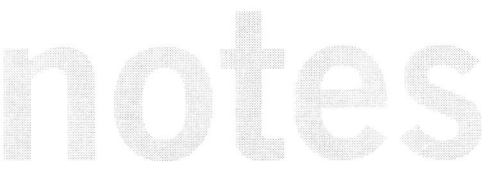

Mythmakers

These are the primary characters who do (or wish to) transform themselves. In so doing, they create a mythical outer persona, which is what others see.

Callie/Cal

Note: when these notes refer to Callie, you will see the use of the female gender. When these notes refer to Cal, the use of the male gender will appear. This difference will reflect the nature of Callie/Cal's duality.

- Calliope, as she is named, refers to the Greek muse of epic poetry and eloquence. This is an interesting overlay to Callie as the narrator/recorder of this story and to the comparative speechlessness of others, specifically her grandfather, Lefty.

- Callie tells us from the beginning that she is born twice: once as an infant and a second time in the hospital after being hit by a tractor. It is only then that she discovers that she is a hermaphrodite. But these are her physical births, preceding her psychological rebirth as a man, which occurs during her time in Zora's house: "*My life during those (nine) months was as divided as my body.*" (p.491)

- Callie, as both a man and a woman, is compassionate, introspective, understanding, and exceptionally mature in her outlook. In her role as observer, she is calm and detailed. Her eyes are the camera that captures the events on behalf of the readers. (see Narrative Voice, p.58)

- Callie's physical nature is the result of destiny, but she debunks the myth that destiny can control us. In the end, Callie takes control of her own destiny. (see Destiny, p.35)

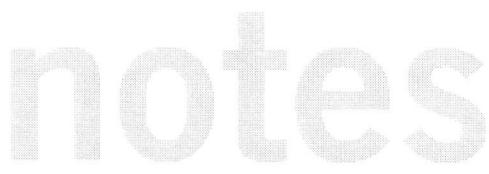

Desdemona

- Desdemona is the family matriarch, who marries Lefty, her brother, who is also her third cousin. They have two children – Milton and Zoë.

- From the Greek origin of her name we know that she is fated for misery. This Desdemona also reminds us of Shakespeare's tragic heroine, who is destroyed by her great love, Othello.

- For a time, she transforms herself into a smart and talented businesswoman who brings the ancient art of silk weaving to the United States.

- Although she commits incest with her brother, she is not condemned by either Eugenides or the reader. She gains our sympathy because she suffers so much from her fear of destiny.

- She is loved and cherished by all, but despite the fact that she is very important to this story she disappears for half the book. Cal describes how he allowed Desdemona to disappear from both the story and his life. This small passage works well on many levels:

    > *Patient reader, you may have been wondering what happened to my grandmother [Desdemona] …. [who] began to fade away …. I allowed Desdemona to slip out of my narrative because … in the dramatic years of my transformation, she slipped out of my attention most of the time.* (p.521)

- It shows that Cal, as the narrator of the story, is clearly in charge of what is or is not included.

- It shows Desdemona's descent into a fog brought on by Alzheimer's or dementia.

- It reflects accurately how most teenagers deal with the senior generations; they usually ignore them and do not see their value until later in adulthood.

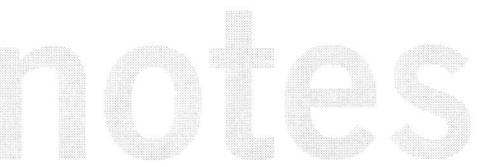

Lefty

- Eluetherios, Desdemona's brother, a.k.a. Lefty, is a gambler whose greatest gamble is his family's genetic dynasty. For a time the odds are in his favor:
    - He earns enough money through gambling to enable them to leave Smyrna for the new world.
    - He and Desdemona marry and have two healthy, normal children.
    - He gambles on people's desire to have liquor despite Prohibition, and he successfully establishes the Zebra Room.
- In the end his luck runs out. Milton's child is born as Callie but is in reality Cal. Lefty gambles away the family fortune and is forced to declare bankruptcy. At the time when Callie is born Lefty suffers a series of strokes, which leave him without the ability to speak.
- Lefty communicates on paper, a theme that Callie/Cal continues as the narrator of this story. **(see Narrative Voice, p.58)** Lefty becomes a translator of Greek myths and legends, an effort that encourages the accessibility of these stories to those who are unfamiliar with them. Callie too is translating for others the unfamiliar story of hermaphrodism.

Milton

- Milton is named for the great Athenian general of the fifth century B.C., who successfully defended the Athenians against a Persian invasion. Our Milton enters the army and also prepares to fight the enemy. Little does he know that the enemy he will face is his own brother-in-law, Father Mike.

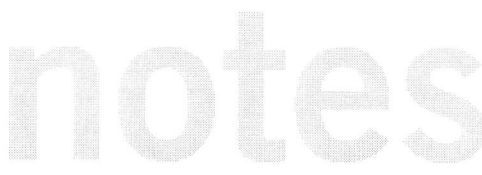

- Milton woos Tessie with his clarinet. The novel's descriptions of Milton's musical flirtation with Tessie are very visual. In cartoon-like imagery, we can almost see the music twirl and swirl out of the mouth of the clarinet and weave its way into Tessie's physical and emotional awareness:

   > *With its fast beat and swirling melody, "Begin the Beguine" rises over the victory garden ... hops the fence ... step[s] around ... climbs the ragged ivy ... up and up it soars.* (p.169)

- Milton is smart, intuitive, and has vision. He builds an empire from hot dogs and provides well for his family. He has successfully taken the first generation (his Greek parents) and transformed it into an American generation (Callie and her brother). (see Transformation, p.33)

- Milton is not interested in his family's past, but he does teach Callie all about Greek myths and legends, especially about the minotaur, another hybrid, consisting of the head of a man and the body of a bull. (see Minotaur and the Maze, p.68)

- Milton travels through the maze of destiny that is handed to him by his family's biological history, by the social environment of his American culture, and by the times in which he lives. His goal is to reach the center of the labyrinth to rescue his daughter without being confronted by the minotaur. He is defeated.

Tessie

- Tessie is the daughter of Sourmelina and Jimmy. Tessie is conceived in the same parallel moment as her husband/cousin, Milton. Here the intermingling and weaving together of the families continues. They have two children, Callie and Chapter 11.

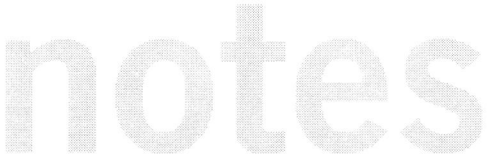

- Tessie, named Theodora, is a lovely human being who adores both her children but especially her daughter. True to her giving and open nature, Tessie is better at accepting Callie's destiny than Milton, who, had he lived, would have been unlikely to understand and accept Cal as he is. He would miss his Callie too much.

- Tessie is the essence of unconditional love, and she has great courage. Although she feels "*crushed by what had happened ... she [intends] to endure it ...*" (p.520)

Sourmelina

- Sourmelina emigrated to the United States before Lefty and Desdemona and gave them the sponsorship they needed to enter the country.

- A cousin to the pair, Sourmelina seems to have an air of mystery about her. There had been rumors of her lesbian affinities, which may have driven her to transform herself in America, the land of opportunity. (see Transformation, p.33)

- She marries Jimmy to legitimize herself but is quite content as a single mother when Jimmy dies and disappears from the scene.

- With Sourmelina, we have yet another "deviation" added to the family mix.

Jimmy/Mr. Fard

- Jimmy, Sourmelina's husband, proves to be the best at transformation. When he disappears under the ice of the Detroit River, we assume, as do all the characters, that he is dead. But since transformation is a major theme in the novel, we should have known that Jimmy would return in some form or another.

- In fact, he returns as a Wizard-of-Oz like character, Mr. Fard. Jimmy is a cat with nine lives; he jumps from one to the other in succession and thus ensures his survival. Mr. Fard gives Desdemona the opportunity to resurrect her skills at making silk. All the characters rethread their lives as smoothly as possible.

Dr. Peter Luce

- Dr. Luce runs the Sexual Disorders and Gender Identity Clinic. If there were a villain in **Middlesex**, it would be Dr. Luce, whose name, like Lucifer's, invokes the idea of malevolent intent. But perhaps Dr. Luce is just a victim of the times.

- He is a leading authority on human hermaphrodism and is writing a paper outlining gender identification for those with androgenital syndrome. (see Identity, p.33) His theory fits into the nature and nurture debate of the sixties and seventies:

    > *In a decade of solid, original research, Luce made his second great discovery: that gender identity is established very early on in life, about the age of two. Gender was like a native tongue; it didn't exist before birth but was imprinted in the brain during childhood, never disappearing. Children learn to speak Male or Female the way they learn to speak English or French.*
    > (p.411)

- Callie can't accept this. Although her upbringing was clearly female, she had always felt clearly male. From her perspective, Luce's diagnosis was a betrayal, especially because he was advocating surgery that would permanently establish Callie as a woman.

Nymphs

These are the objects of Cal's affection. The dictionary defines nymph as a "mythological semi-divine spirit regarded as a maiden and associated with an aspect of nature, especially rivers and woods." By this definition, Callie is also a nymph. Our Callie is unmasked in the woods, both behind the Obscure Object's country house and again in the forested park in San Francisco. It is only after Callie is reborn as Cal that he is ready to seek and accept a real, non-mythical love object – Julie.

Clementine

- Callie meets Clementine Stark when she's seven years old. At the sophisticated age of eight, Clementine is more sexually aware than Callie and wants to practice kissing. This is the beginning of the awakening of Callie's sexuality. However, at the time, no one realizes that for Callie, Clementine is the opposite sex:

    > *And then, somewhere below ... my heart reacting. Not a thump exactly. Not even a leap. But a kind of swish, like a frog kicking off from a muddy bank ... I tried to hold up my end of things. But Clementine was way ahead of me. She swiveled her head back and forth the way actresses did in the movies. I started doing the same, but out of the corner of her mouth she scolded, "You're the man."* (p.265)

- And indeed, Callie is the man.

The Obscure Object

- When the Obscure Object walks into Callie's eighth-grade class, she walks straight into Callie's heart. By calling her the Obscure Object, Callie is referring to a 1977 film, *That Obscure Object of Desire*, where the film's hero is love struck by a beautiful girl and follows her around while carrying a heavy sack over his shoulder:

    > *That was exactly how I felt, following my own Obscure Object. As though I were carrying around a mysterious, unexplained burden or weight. I'm going to call her that ... I'm going to call her the Obscure Object. For sentimental reasons. (I also have to protect her identity.)* (p.325)

- Cal is also sentimentally protective of his own sexual identity, especially later when it comes to his relationship with Julie.

- The Obscure Object is interested in a good-looking boy, Rex Reese. Her brother, Jerome, is interested in Callie. Callie's angst-ridden description of this pre-teen foray into sex is both poignant, conflicted, funny, and sad. It should remind the readers of the memories of their own initial sexual adventures or misadventures.

- Callie and the Obscure Object become friends, first emotionally and then sexually. The deliberate act of not identifying the Obscure Object shows clearly that she, like Callie, is also at the emergence of an unclear sexual identity. She may go either way, and it is this choice that Callie is protecting.

- Until Cal emerges from the barbershop as a boy, she is her own Obscure Object. Never comfortable with her sexuality, she now works hard to adopt the characteristics, such as walking with a male swagger, that must accompany her new identity.

Julie

- Julie is a beautiful Asian woman, a photographer, and a cyclist, with whom Cal falls in love. His feelings for Julie are clearly not ambiguous, but he proceeds cautiously so as not to be hurt by rejection.

- Julie disappears and reappears whenever Cal, the narrator, returns to the present time. (see Narrative Voice, p.58)

- Her photography is important, not only for the observant qualities of this profession, but also for the fact that Julie photographs factories; this ties together Berlin and Detroit.

- These two places are industrial cities in an industrial age. It is hard to see the fine points below the output of smog by the factory chimneys. A photograph concentrates on the details of the outer structure while capturing the building's character. So too does Cal concentrate on the details of his outer structure while capturing the complex character hidden beneath. (see Home Movies, p.61)

The Chorus

The chorus is made up of the rest of the surrounding characters, who affect the main characters in some way.

The function of the chorus in Greek drama is to comment on and interpret the actions of the main characters. In the context of this novel, Eugenides uses the chorus as a backdrop against which the main characters are reflected. In other words, we see what our characters are dealing with and how they handle themselves.

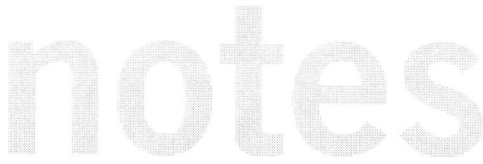

Chapter 11

- Callie's brother is the only other un-named character in the novel. His nickname is an in-joke. Chapter 11 is a term that refers to the United States Bankruptcy Protection Act. In the novel, Callie's Chapter 11 ends up taking over the family business and, yes, like his grandfather before him, he runs it into the ground.

- Chapter 11 is not as much a contrast to Callie through personality as he is another example of a product of his times. He drops out and turns on, just as millions of young people did in the sixties. Eugenides highlights the era in which this story takes place.

- Chapter 11 may not be the ideal son or grandson, but he comes through for Cal in the end. He accepts him unconditionally.

Zoë/Father Mike

- Michael Antoniou, who lives in Lina's boarding house while studying to be a priest, falls in love with Tessie and eventually marries Aunt Zoë, Milton's sister. But first Tessie becomes engaged to Father Mike, because as Callie says, *"Maybe my mother, having grown up without a father, was trying to marry one."* (p.181)

- Father Mike is the unintended recipient of the proof of Callie's sex. At her baptism, Callie hits Father Mike right between the eyes when she pees on him. Had anyone been sufficiently observant, it might have been noticed that the trajectory of this reverse and unwanted baptism formed an arc, which boys make when they pee, in contrast to the straight-line stream of urine that girls make.

- As Callie tells us, *"... no one wondered about the engineering involved."* (p.222) From this moment on, Father Mike locks himself in a one-sided competition with Milton. (see Milton, p.20)

Rex Reese and Jerome

- Rex Reese, boyfriend of the Obscure Object, sounds as if he should have come out of a comic book. He is as self-absorbed as only a teenaged boy can be. But it is Jerome who is truly comically funny as he makes a pass at Callie and succeeds in penetrating her. He is so happy that he "made it" that he hasn't noticed Callie's unusual structure.

- Adolescence is a time where ideas form, identity is forged, and philosophy is sculptured. It is a time to try new things, especially in the dark, which symbolically represents the unknown.

- After a series of dramatic events involving these four adolescents, there is a minor accident, which lands Callie in the hospital. It is there that Callie is "re-born" and "re-identified" as a male.

Bob Presto/Zora

- Bob Presto gives Cal a job doing live erotic shows in his after-hours sex club. It is here that Cal meets Zora, also a hermaphrodite. Zora has Androgen Insensitivity, which means her body has developed along female lines but has no womb or ovaries. Like Cal, she also does not think of herself as a woman.

- Zora educates Cal about the history of hermaphrodites and gives Cal a balanced perspective from which to view himself. She speaks of the hermaphrodite, in Platonic and Jungian terms, as the original person made up of two halves – one male, one female.

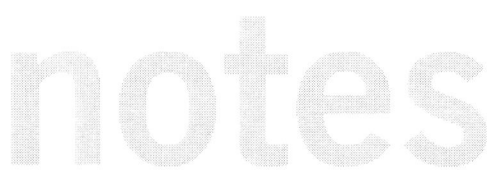

- Bob Presto and Zora enable Callie to come to terms with her sexuality. As distasteful as the thought is of Callie doing erotic shows in Bob Presto's club, this is the bottom of the pool from which Callie must rise.

- Bob's name evokes the magic of transformation that each hermaphrodite hopes to go through. Through Cal's experience at the club, Presto indirectly helps Cal solidify his position in the world as a male.

FOCUS POINTS AND THEMES

Transformation and Identity

Fate and Destiny vs. Chance

The Creation Story, Original Sin

Duality

Punishment and Crime

Time

Writing Process

FOCUS POINTS AND THEMES

Transformation and Identity
physical change, coming-of-age, redefinition

The subject matter of the novel, hermaphrodism, forces the reader to acknowledge and accept what has been swept under society's rug.

- On a smaller scale, Cal's adolescent struggle for sexual, personal, and gender identification parallels the struggle of every single teenager and is reminiscent of Holden Caulfield in **Catcher in the Rye**. Cal's struggle is a metaphor for every kind of change, mutation, adaptation, and alteration in life: immigrant adaptation, national and cultural adaptation, and gender confusion. These all make an appearance in this book.

- The American dream is part of this saga of transformation, but the melting-pot syndrome only melts the first layer. As Desdemona finds out, her efforts to reinvent herself as Lefty's wife falter; there are always traces of the original situation left behind, and they can show up in very unattractive and transformed ways – for example, in Cal's genetic history.

- Everyone switches identity:
    - Cal switches sexual identity;
    - Lefty and Desdemona switch familial identity;
    - Jimmy Zizmo switches personal identity.

- When Cal and his brother drive through the streets of Detroit after Milton's death, Cal remarks that it is amazing that the world contains so many different lives with so many stories and challenges, each one struggling with life until the moment of death:

    I was thinking how amazing it was that the world contained so many lives ...

    What really mattered in life, what gave it weight, was death. Seen this way, my bodily metamorphosis was a small event. (p.518, 519)

- The truth of his thoughts is that each life has the same characteristics that define all human beings, yet each one is unique. Each one transforms physically, psychologically, and spiritually in its own way. Because each life ends at the same place, what matters is the process of life, not the problems and the judgments made by others along the way. Perhaps what is abnormal is really normal.

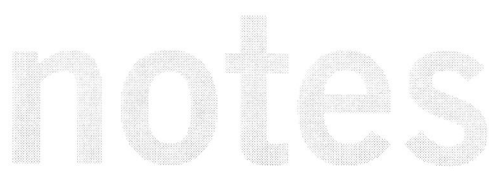

Fate and Destiny vs. Chance and Choice

Life started out one thing and then suddenly turned a corner and became something else. (p.519)

- The nature vs. nurture followers entered the destiny vs. choice debate in the sixties and seventies when society was encouraged to abandon the idea of fate and gender differences. The belief was that you could mold an innocent psyche into whatever shape you wished: girls could play with trucks, boys with dolls, and there would be no adverse consequences: *"Free will [was] making a comeback. Biology gives you a brain. Life turns it into a mind."* (p.479)

- This contradicted some of the great thinking that came before. In his reflective piece, "Symposium," Plato had put forward the theory that every person was originally made up of equal parts, male and female, but these parts were later separated by the gods, who liked to be in control of human destiny.

- In the early twentieth century, the psychologist Jung continued to investigate the two subconscious halves of the human psyche – animus and anima. His theory of the collective unconscious also addresses the fact that humans are pre-programmed. (Eugenides uses the term "preformation.")

- How big a part does choice play in our lives? According to Eugenides, both viewpoints are valid. (see Creation Story, next page) If you deliberately play the wrong card, the gods will get you every time. One never knows how or when the retribution will come – it is written in the wind or on the genes, as it were. Lefty and Desdemona cheated society's prohibition against the marriage of siblings. Despite the fact that they are brother and sister, they are also third cousins. The inbreeding in their small town will eventually show up as Cal, the hermaphrodite. There is always a cost to cheating the gods.

- Genetic stew is what is served in this novel. With this menu, what chance does Cal have?

  Sourmelina Zizmo (nee Pappasdiamondopoulis) wasn't only my first cousin twice removed. She was also my grandmother. My father was his own mother's (and father's) nephew. In addition to being my grandparents, Desdemona and Lefty were my great-aunt and -uncle. My parents were my second cousins and Chapter Eleven was my third cousin as well as my brother. (p.198) (see Grandpa's Song, p.77)

- However, armed with the strength of her ancestors and their ability to transform themselves, Callie takes control of her own fate and turns to face her destiny. Physically Cal will always be a hermaphrodite, but he accepts and recognizes his sexual identity and uses that confirmation to go on to live a productive life. Callie finds her own way out of the maze of the minotaur.

The Creation Story and Original Sin

In both Christianity and in Greek mythology, the sins of the parents may be visited upon the children.

- Greek myths highlight the idea that the gods are as fallible as humans. When either makes a mistake, there is always a consequence. Furthermore, Greek mythology shows humans to be their own enemies because they think themselves to be as good as the gods. This is a punishable offense, and retribution is swift.

- In Christianity, the concept of original sin is also an all-encompassing philosophy that defines the whole of human experience as inescapable from its fate, but while Greek mythology intermingles

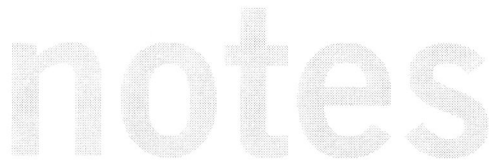

gods and humans, Christian philosophy separates them and introduces the idea of individual free will and human responsibility.

- The theory of preformation, as explained in the novel on pages 198 to 200, states that everything already exists; it is simply hidden, unseen, or is in miniature form and needs to be expanded. In her wonderful book, **The Mark of the Angel,** Nancy Huston also talks about this notion. She says that we knew everything *"before we were born ... then [we] forgot ... [and we] had to learn all over again."*
(See the Bookclub-in-a-Box discussion guide for this novel.)

- Although the novel concentrates on fate and predetermined genetics, it still leaves room for the possibility of free will. While there may be no way to avoid what has been preformed, there is choice in our reactions and our deeds. Eugenides makes a case for both destiny and free will to co-exist. People are given pre-determined destinies, but they can choose what to use: *"Fate or luck had brought me here and I had to take from it what I needed."* (Cal, p.489) Callie makes her choice.

- Callie is again reborn in the barbershop. What emerges from under the scissors is *"not the shy girl with the tangled black hair in her face, but instead her fraternal twin brother ... I was a new creation."* (p.445)

Duality

Duality in life is represented by many things in the novel, but its central image, hermaphrodism, is the spark for this discussion. Eugenides talks about it this way:

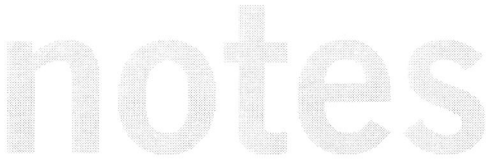

- We understand reproduction as two people who come together to create a new person, either male or female. However, the laws of nature have complicated the common understanding of this by sometimes throwing a curve into the mixture. As a result, it is possible to have a person born with both male and female sex organs: a new entity, known as a hermaphrodite. Although this may seem out of the norm, it is a natural and not a man-made phenomenon.

- As Cal learns from Zora, history, literature, and drama have long recorded the existence of a third gender, which, like Cal, is "... *special, exalted, endowed with mystical gifts*." (p.495) This reinforces Plato's theory of separation. (see Fate, p.35)

- According to Carl Jung, everyone's psyche possesses both genders, and it is up to us to integrate both sides. (see Jung, p.78) This parallels the physical duality of hermaphrodism:

    The original person was two halves, one male, one female. Then these got separated. That's why everybody's always searching for their other half. Except for us. We've got both halves already. (p.489)

- Blends are normal; hybrids are normal. Nature is filled with cross-pollination and new species. Callie is simply another species.

- A physical symbol of this duality is Berlin, the home-place of both Cal and Eugenides – a once-divided city is now unified once more.

    Once again, in Berlin, a Stephanides lives among Turks ... We're all made up of many parts, other halves. Not just me. (p.440)

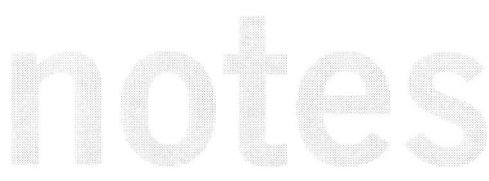

Punishment and Crime

In Greek tragedy, crime is committed when humans try to take control of their destiny instead of leaving it in the hands of the gods. The gods always promise retribution, perhaps not immediately, but eventually and certainly.

- Desdemona and Lefty's crime is to marry despite the fact that they are brother and sister:

    > ... *punishment for her crime was going to be taken out in the most devastating way possible: not on her own soul but in the bodies of her children.* (p.157)

- Cal is Desdemona's grandchild; the sins of the grandparents are now visible. Ironically, and humorously, when Desdemona finds out that Cal is a hermaphrodite, she is not upset, but rather she feels vindicated that her spoon was correct – that Cal is a boy, which was the destiny that Desdemona had predicted for him.

- When Milton goes off to war, Desdemona feels that *"God has brought the judgment down on us that we deserve."* (p.194) Desdemona tries to bargain with heaven. She wants an exemption from the military for Milton (p.191) and in exchange for his safety she promises God that Milton will fix the church in Bithynios.

- Desdemona asks for two things: in addition to the exemption for Milton, she seeks redemption for her own sins. Milton never keeps the promise and in the end is duly punished, perhaps for both of them.

- Although this seems to contradict what Eugenides is presenting, it does not. What appears as punishment is merely destiny; fate is what is in our control. Callie decides what to do with her destiny and makes her choices accordingly.

    > *Fate or luck had brought me here and I had to take from it what I needed.* (p.489)

Time

The British author and poet Austin Dobson (1840-1921) talks of time in his work "The Paradox of Time:"

> *Time goes, you say? Ah, no!*
> *Alas, Time stays, we go.*

- In his novel, Eugenides uses time in this sense. As readers, we are given the impression that it is not time that is moving, but that there is a panorama of characters, scenes, and situations parading before us. Life is the microfiche machine that Eugenides sat in front of for hours while researching his story.

- The novel's narration moves back and forth in time, even while simultaneously advancing the story. There is also the more-than-occasional pause to visually record a scene, an encounter, or an emotion. (see Home Movies, p.61)

- Eugenides uses his narrative like a hand-held camera, complete with director's cuts and fast scene changes. The camera is never out of focus, but the characters may not always see things clearly:

    > *Despite my grandmother's corrective lenses, the world remained out of focus.* (p.171)

    > *.... Though the army helmet obscured Milton's present vision, it gave him a pretty good picture of the future.*
    > (Milton - p.186)

- Time is a central theme in the novel and it unfolds, in another sense, like an advancing glacier: it is slow, inevitable, and unstoppable. Genetics and destiny can be viewed the same way. The view of the ancient Greeks is that once the seed is sown, it will eventually appear. In the case of this novel, Callie is the surface on which the gene is written.

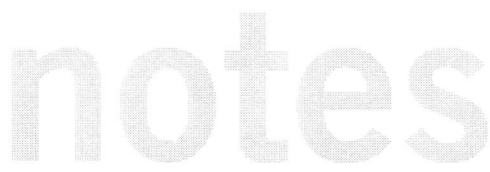

- Much of the story's action is told as an unfolding sequence, but occasionally Eugenides speeds it up, using time-lapse narration as if it were time-lapse photography. This adds to the feeling that the reader is watching a drama on stage, all the while knowing that other actions are taking place behind the scenes: *"... let me fill you in on what has happened these last eleven years."* (p.168)

Writing Process

Fiction vs. Faction – Writing vs. Reality

- A factual, non-fictional exploration of hermaphrodism would explain this condition in a clear and definitive manner, but it would not uncover the human essence of this unusual biological situation. Eugenides uses the writing process to creatively address the topic from a level of emotional truth. He believes that the novelist can only go into the minds and hearts of characters of either gender if he/she is a hermaphrodite of sorts. Cal is the writer's perfect narrative choice.

- The writing process of the novel consciously demonstrates the theme of debate: nature vs. nurture, roots vs. rootlessness, fate vs. chance, reality vs. illusion. Eugenides uses the previously undiscussed and non-discussable subject of sexual aberration as a jumping-off point to open the conversation.

- In addition to being the narrator, Cal is also a writer creating his own Greek myth, a tale told to explain the unexplainable.

- By so doing, Cal explores the themes of gender identity, cultural identity, what society will and won't accept, and to what degree. He surveys the legitimacy of the narrative voice and how it can best investigate the novel's questions. In other words, he gives the reader a perspective that gives the best answers.

- Cal is the unsurpassed choice for the narrative voice because, in addition to everything else, he embodies, literally and figuratively, the cross-cultural nature of America. Upon Milton's death, Cal writes, *"A real Greek might end on this tragic note, but an American is inclined to stay upbeat."* (p.511) Cal is both.

- Another of the points Eugenides makes is that not everything is as it appears on paper.

    o When Callie is encouraged by Dr. Luce to keep a journal, she fictionalizes her feelings to fit his expectations: "... *it was amazing how it worked: the tiniest bit of truth made credible the greatest lies."* (p.418)

    o Callie does not know it, but Tessie's letters to Father Mike during the war, were *"wholesale fictions"* designed to prove that *"real life doesn't live up to writing about it ..."* (p.189)

    o Seeing how her own fictionalization succeeds, what is she to believe when she researches a dictionary entry for her condition and ends up with a synonym of "monster" for hermaphrodite?

    > *Here was a book that contained the collected knowledge of the past while giving evidence of present social conditions.* (p.431)

    o Callie reads Dr. Luce's final report. Although she knows that she gave him false directions for his findings, nevertheless she feels betrayed. The report states that because Callie has been thoroughly raised as a girl, she must have surgery to complete the transformation. She is shocked and devastated.

- In this way, Eugenides firmly confronts the concept of the "book" as a source of unchallenged authority. Perhaps this relates to the greatest written source in history, the Bible, which is, as a rule, accepted unconditionally. When Callie finds the description of herself as a monster in a library book, she accepts it without question because it has come closest to matching her own feelings about herself. She is looking straight into the eyes of the hideous minotaur, the monster of Crete, herself. Callie becomes frightened and runs away.

- But mostly Eugenides is interested in using good old-fashioned storytelling to get his points across. The act of telling stories is a purely human activity:

    That's how people live ... by telling stories ... that's how we understand who we are, where we come from. Stories are everything .... It's the greatest story ever told. (p.179) (Notice the movie title.)

- Again, it is Callie who points out the purpose and advantage of storytelling. Cal's adult journal is the final step in the writing process, as Eugenides sees it. Cal informs us, as readers, that it is through stories that we learn about others and about ourselves. Even when stories have many different perspectives and different outcomes, contrived or coincidental, it does not matter. It is the tale that is to be appreciated and enjoyed.

WRITING STRUCTURE

The Greek Card
Greek Gifts
The History Card
Parallel Suits

WRITING STRUCTURE

Like Lefty, Eugenides is a crafty gambler who also plays a competent game of cards. Using the gambling motif, Eugenides builds the tension by keeping his cards close to his chest and playing them one by one as needed.

The Greek Card

- This Greek-American saga dabbles in epic poetry:
    - Calliope is named for the muse of epic poetry.
    - There is a Greek chorus of supporting voices. **(see Chorus, p.26)** Callie is most often her own chorus, and we do see her as others reflect her.
    - Greek mythology, with its emphasis on incest, metamorphosis, and other dramatic events is central to this novel.
    - In addition, there is the hand of fate or the fateful hand of the gods, which punishes human pride. For example, there are Desdemona and Lefty, who thought they could get away with marriage.
    - Like Theseus in the minotaur's maze, Callie is caught in a maze made by the people around her. She struggles to find her way out, even as others, including her loved ones, are struggling to keep her in. **(see Minotaur and the Maze, p.68)**

- The significance of Greek myth and legend is not lost on either Eugenides or the reader. These myths and legends form the structural foundation of everything we know in the world today. After Greek mythology, the Bible comes in second.

- These stories continue to move readers because their themes are timeless. The Greek imagination concentrated on man's philosophical search for excellence and perfection. The tales championed the physical body, the human mind, and the human spirit and believed that each of these could continually strive for brilliance and distinction. It was a natural leap of connection, therefore, to consider gods as pseudo-humans, rather than the other way around. This is why the gods, in these stories, are so all-powerful.

The Gifts of Greek Mythology

- Stories, literature – many words have their origin in Greek mythology, even slang terms, e.g., "by jove," and "by heck".

- Music, art, theater inspired by Greek mythology.

- Sport, Olympics – idea of competition, names: Argonauts, marathon, Achilles.

- Calendar – terminology – the names of the days and the ideas behind the months, year, and seasons.

- Solar system – names of the planets and stars.

- Chemistry – names of some of the substances, e.g., mercury, plutonium, uranium.

- Manufacturing and business – take their own names and give their products names from mythology to give a superhuman dimension to their essence. For example, Nike is the Greek goddess of victory.

- Geographic terms – geography, ocean, atlas.

- Botany – names of plants and flowers, e.g., narcissus, iris, hyacinth, rose.

- Figures of speech – Achilles heel, Herculean task, Midas touch, etc.

The World History Card

- **Middlesex** is ambitiously set in America in the last century, where it touches on a variety of topics: immigration (three generations of a Greek-American family), Prohibition, the Depression, World War II, the Civil Rights movement, the new automobile industry, the rise of organized labor, the OPEC oil crisis, and even September 11.

- The Nation of Islam (see Fard, p.75) was founded in 1932 by a man who was neither white nor black. (At that time, Greeks were not considered white.) The founder, a man of unknown origins, had previously worked in the silk trade and had spoken publicly about racial origins and genetic transformations. This detail works its way perfectly into the novel when Desdemona is looking for a job and when Jimmy Zizmo needs a place to hide.

- Eugenides paints a vivid picture of the socio-cultural times of the seventies, which includes icons like Jerry Garcia and the Grateful Dead, and the emergence of the idea of unisex.

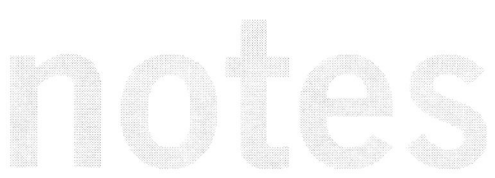

Parallel Suits

There are many examples of parallelism, juxtaposition, symmetry, and simply unbelievable coincidence, which tend to stretch our imagination and therefore tend to test our acceptance of the truth. Eugenides is emphasizing the idea of perspective. What one believes depends on who is doing the believing and the range of his/her experience.

- One such example is the likelihood of Tessie and Milton being conceived at the same moment on the same night and who later marry.
- Desdemona escapes the destruction of Smyrna in 1922 but eventually retires to Smyrna Beach, Florida.
- Milton and Tessie have a child of true "middlesex," one who is born a girl but is really a boy. This family finds a house on Middlesex Street. This same girl/boy, Cal, later moves to Berlin, a city that itself was divided in half at one time.
- Fire is what drives Lefty and Desdemona out of Smyrna and into the arms of America, the free; fire drives Milton out of his inner city Detroit restaurant into the bosom of Grosse Pointe, the snobby.
- Desdemona, the expert Smyrna silk maker, ends up teaching silk making at the Muslim center in central Detroit. In a Wizard-of-Oz-like appearance, she comes to learn that Mr. Fard is really Jimmy transformed.

Coincidences like these are the kind of thing only real life can come up with. Truth is stranger than fiction, except when it's fiction imitating true life.

There are many examples of analogy, common-day references placed together – not juxtaposed, but simply together on the same plate.

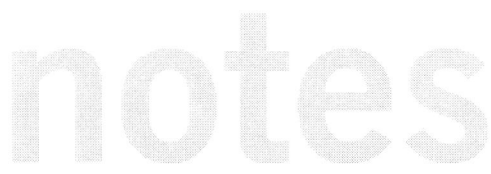

- For example, there are three dominant birth images in the novel, all of which involve Detroit: the birthplace of the auto industry, the birthplace of Cal, and the birthplace of the Nation of Islam. They are not juxtaposed but are linked with the same silk thread.

- Cal, living as an adult in Berlin, undergoes the same *"struggle for unification, for Einheit"* (p.106) as the city.

- Cal weaves his story with a silken thread. Although the reader sometimes can't see it, Cal never loses the thread. This web has no loose connections.

- There are many parallel stories that play against each other: Lefty/Desdemona, Milton/Tessie, Father Mike/Tessie, Zoë/Father Mike, Jimmy/Lina, Cal and his many loves.

- Julie, the photographer, takes photos of factories; Detroit is the factory capital of the world.

- We are constantly reminded of everyone's two sides. For example, Desdemona as a vibrant young woman is hardly recognizable in the older stereotypical caricature of herself.

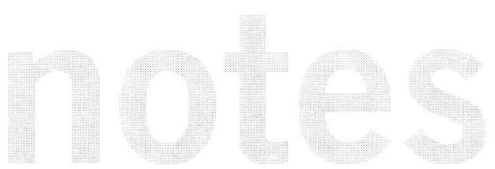

WRITING STYLE

Layers

Language, Literary Reference

Narrative Voice

Humor, Observation

Home Movies

WRITING STYLE

Jeffrey Eugenides is a very considerate writer, both to his characters and to his readers; both are treated with respect. He introduces us to facts and ideas that would normally make us uncomfortable, but because of his warm, friendly tone, we relax and are more open to hear what he has to say.

Here, Eugenides utilizes the Greek formula of transformation – the style is true to the form of the novel's themes. The narrator switches from child to adult, from innocence to sophistication, from female to male. Each transition is essential to the story and is intricately woven into the story's fabric.

Notwithstanding the fact that **Middlesex** has won a twenty-first-century prize, it is written more in the style of an epic novel like **Anna Karenina,** or **A Fine Balance.** (See the Bookclub-in-a-Box discussion guide for Mistry's novel.) It takes time to draw in the details of the surrounding environment, the people, and the events of the day, and Eugenides does a masterful job.

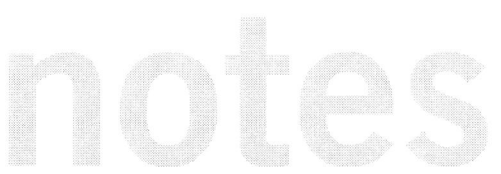

Layers

Eugenides' style and structure intertwine smoothly. His story is well constructed, detailed, and delicately woven, yet it is accessible to every reader because of its tone. With his straightforward, honest, and sympathetic approach, we become highly involved with the characters.

- The finely layered story tastes like a sweet baklava with its paper-thin phyllo pastry. All the historical details are intermingled throughout the story – they are real details. Art imitates life. (see Background Information, p.73)

- Throughout the story Eugenides builds on the reader's skepticism of Cal's condition. It's hard to know what to believe. The story moves back and forth like the swish of Zora's fish tail. This tall tale, like most myths and legends, requires us to swallow the fish whole. Eugenides makes this point through the trucker who picks up the runaway Cal and tells him a whole slew of believe-it-or-not stories. (p.447)

- By the time we learn the details of Cal's syndrome and its possible outcome we are hooked on the story, the characters, the details, and the probabilities. We are delighted to accept the challenge of fiction reflecting strange truth.

There are four balanced sections in the novel, each dealing with a different aspect of Cal. In books one and two, we learn about his psychological, physical, and cultural pre-history, first through the story of his grandparents, then his parents. In books three and four, we see Cal's changes, first as a girl, then as a boy.

- These are all variations on a theme or different models of the same basic car. Eugenides is continually shifting gears between the past, the present, and the future. The car image is appropriate given the setting, Detroit, and Milton's love of cars.

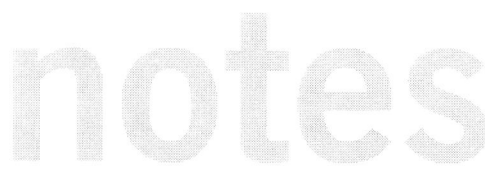

- The four books in the novel represent Jung's four stages of consciousness as well as the life cycle (birth, childhood, adulthood, death).

Language

Eugenides plays with language and loves to make up words.

- Lefty opens the Zebra Room and learns to "*[channel] his intellectual powers into the science of mixology.*" (p.132) Ironically, he already has a part in mixology when he and Desdemona combine their genes and have a family.

- It takes some time, but for Desdemona, who works in the Muslim Girls Training School, this means that she is becoming a true Detroiter. She is fascinated by Fard's voice and his message on behalf of black people. It is then that Desdemona begins to see "*everything in terms of black and white.*" (p.156) This is not hard to do in a city like Detroit, which has population that is racially mixed.

Literary Reference

- In T.S. Eliot's poem "The Waste Land," The Fire Sermon talks about "*Mr. Eugenides, the Smyrna merchant*" who invites Tiresias, "*though blind, throbbing between two lives, Old man with wrinkled female breasts*" to lunch. The coincidence of the name that Eliot uses for his poem and Eugenides' real name is startling. Jeffrey Eugenides admits that this happenstance gave him the final push to write this story. He uses Cal as Tiresias.

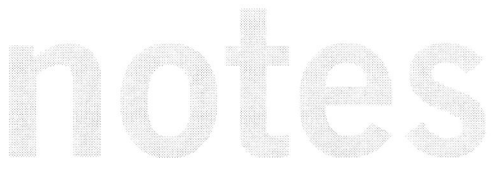

- Eugenides uses the story of Tiresias (see p.74) to show why Cal, as the narrator, is able to see events not only in the future but in the past before he was born. Like Tiresias, Cal is omniscient. He knows things that he cannot possibly know. But like all narrators, fiction or otherwise, Cal invents his own story in order to understand himself better. We are all our own prophets, masters of our own fates (not destiny). Eugenides gives Callie the role of Tiresias twice: once in the school play and once in the play of her own life.

Narrative Voice

- The progress of the narration in this novel is unusual. The novel is told with the innocence of a narrator who learns what is happening at the same time as the reader. Yet Cal tells the story from his memory and seems to unfold it in real-time. Cal's innocence takes us into the story's future while simultaneously revealing the story's past.

- The writing style is linear yet interrupted. Cal constantly uses flash forward, a technique for letting us know what will happen later. Flash forward differs from the literary technique of foreshadowing. With the former we get real details as to the future; with foreshadowing, clues are embedded in the narrative, which we may or may not see on the first reading.

   Are we reading the signs correctly? Do we believe in the ultimate truth of Desdemona's spoon?

- The narration is not in the style of a journal or diary. Cal interacts directly with the readers and often addresses us personally as "dear reader." This is done in the style of Nabokov, the Russian writer, who openly discusses his themes while they are playing themselves out in his fiction. Callie /Cal does the same.

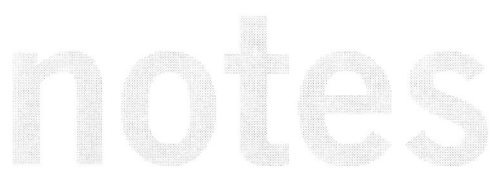

- Eugenides has fun with the narrative voice and its sound. We hear Cal's voice before he/she is born. The lapse of time in the structure is an effective technique that allows the reader to fall in love with Callie the minute she's born. We know her; we like her; we buy her story. She has become part of us, the dear readers.

- Even though there is one narrative voice, there are always two viewpoints in the presentation. Callie feels like Tiresias: first she is one thing, and then she is another. Cal is the balance to Callie's perspective.

- Most of the time Cal narrates from his/her own standpoint. Occasionally, Cal admits that he must enter into the mind of one of the other characters in the guise of the omniscient narrator. He is claiming writer-character privilege: *"... now I have to enter Father Mike's head ... I feel myself being sucked in and I can't resist."* (p.509) At other times, Cal claims he cannot enter the thoughts of another. **(See Writing Process, p.41)**

- The essence of fiction is in the make-believe of its form. It is a creation of the author's imagination and, in essence, is a lie. Yet truth in fiction is what all readers relate to. Eugenides is continually referring to fiction in terms of truth, lies, and possibilities: *"It would be a lie to tell you I understood everything I was feeling. You don't, at fourteen."* (p.449)

  At the same time, Callie calls upon our empathetic understanding of her situation in order to confirm our acceptance of her/him as an authoritative narrator.

- The use of the present tense in the narration of the past helps to intermingle past, present, and future throughout the novel. A Jungian concept is relevant here: you can't understand the present or the future without knowing the past.

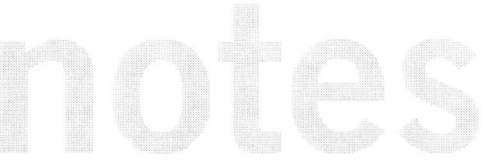

- Cal interrupts his own narrative with a seemingly out-of-place account of his relationship with Julie. It is out of place for many reasons:
    - It is passionless and often pointless. These interruptions come in the middle of dramatic descriptions or occurrences. The last one (p.513-514) comes between Milton's death and his funeral. But life is like that – there are always disruptions and interruptions.
    - Although we like to know that Cal is eventually happy in a relationship, the purpose of these pauses is to remind us to look to the future, to anticipate the unknown.
    - Eugenides also emphasizes that not everything in life may prove to be exciting, but it can be comforting and acceptable. This last point is especially pertinent to the main idea of the novel. Eugenides is presenting hermaphrodism as neither new nor unusual; it should attract no special attention. The main message of the novel is to emphasize how this syndrome should be considered just another normal aspect of the abnormality of humanity.

Humor

- The humor in the novel ranges from soft puns and word plays to laugh-out-loud pleasure. Eugenides uses his offbeat sense of humor to establish a balance for a subject that feels too serious to discuss.
- The car chase between Milton's American-dream Cadillac and Father Mike's Grecian-green Gremlin is an example:

    It wasn't like a car chase in the movies. There was no swerving, no near collisions. It was, after all, a car chase between a Greek Orthodox priest and a middle-aged Republican. (p.505)

The car chase ends a life as well as a lifelong relationship. This is serious business and is highlighted, but not diminished, by the sardonic humor of the description.

- Canadian connection: This very small aside from the action of the novel points again to the merging of two things, in this case a continent shared by two countries that are similar yet different. (p.507)

Detailed Observation

- There is beautiful, detailed and visually clever description: *"To anyone who never personally experienced it, it's difficult to describe the ominous, storm-gathering quality of my grandmother's fanning."* (p.219) Desdemona has a set of six souvenir fans, each relaying a different aspect of Turkish atrocities toward the Greeks – *"a collector's set."*

Home Movies

- The opening chapter of section three of the novel is called "Home Movies". The entire novel, **Middlesex**, is a film, a home movie devoted to the characters Eugenides has lovingly created. But Eugenides is a better photographer than Milton. He has created not just a home movie, but a real film with a visually rich sense of exploration. The camera zooms in and out, pans the scenery or focuses on a single moment.

- This extremely visual novel is its own movie. Cal is the literal and visual recorder and holds both his pen and a camera at the same time. Much of his description follows the camera's eye, and we see a lovely pan of the scene before we hear the dialogue or see the action. First he sets up the scene and then he zooms in. Often the technique is identical to time-lapse photography, where we see the rose unfold in thirty seconds when the real time span is hours. (see Time, p.40)

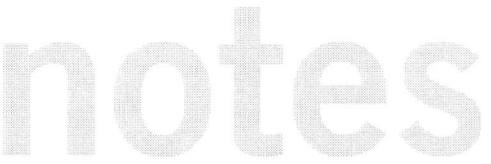

- In another example, the ransom scene (p.502) is filmed in pink light, with full directorial comments. As explained by Cal, pink lights are not a natural phenomenon anywhere outside of Detroit. People in Detroit are familiar with the effect produced by the combined reflection of chemicals in the air. As a result, *"the entire Detroit sky would [then reflect] the soft pink of cotton candy."* (p.502) Like everything else in the novel, this is not a normal event to the world at large, but is natural to those who live in Detroit. Point taken once again.

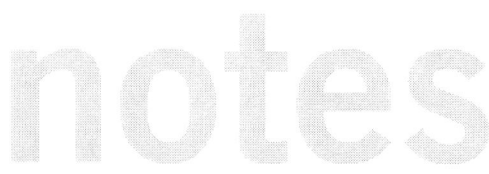

SYMBOLS

Silk, Chekhov Gun

Zora's Diary, Hermaphroditus

Water and the Bridge

Minotaur and the Maze

Gambling, Numbers

SYMBOLS

Silk

For his theme of metamorphosis, Eugenides avoids the usual symbol of transformation, the butterfly, and uses instead the silkworm. It fulfills all the requirements of this literary theme: the silkworm goes through some radical changes from infancy to adulthood and, in fact, changes form completely.

- So too do all adolescents, including and especially Cal. Callie changes not only into an adult but changes from a female into a male. This transformation is not easy but is as strong and sure as a strand of silk.

Chekhov's Gun

- As a symbol, this one is deliberately subtle. Sitting on the wall the gun is innocent, but we are all familiar with its power. There is great tension in waiting for the gun to be fired, and when it is, the tremendous noise that shatters the silence is shocking.

- Eugenides doesn't overwork this symbol – it is mentioned only twice: once when the gun is noticed and once when it actually goes off. The gun is a symbol for Cal:

  > *I can't help thinking about that storytelling precept as I contemplate the gun beneath my father's pillow.* (p.236)

  > *Chekhov was right. If there's a gun on the wall, it's got to go off. In real life, however, you never know where the gun is hanging. The gun my father kept under his pillow never fired a shot. The rifle over the Object's mantel never did either. ... But in the emergency room things were different ... the way the doctor and nurse reacted made it clear that my body had lived up to the narrative requirements.* (p.396)

Zora's Diary

- Zora's diary is modeled after Michele Foucault's translated account of Herculine Barbin, which in turn was modeled after Alexina Barbin, the French hermaphrodite writer of a nineteenth-century diary. There is a universal fascination and curiosity about a character who is able to live both male and female lives at once. Zora also tries to raise awareness of the issue.

Hermaphroditus

- Hermaphroditus was the son of Hermes (the messenger of the gods) and Aphrodite (the goddess of love). Hermaphroditus became involved with a nymph who loved him and was joined with her into a single bisexual person. (See Hermaphrodism, p.73)

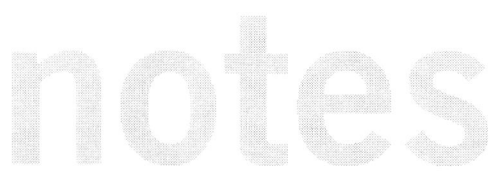

- As a symbol, the hermaphrodite is mythical in nature and so provides Eugenides with the perfect metaphorical material within which to wrap Cal. This includes the Greek gods and goddesses, the silkworm, and Tiresias.

Water and the Bridge

- Water plays an important part in the novel, and so does the bridge that spans it.
    - Desdemona and Lefty cross the ocean between the old world and the new.
    - Jimmy "dies" in the water.
    - Cal is reborn in the water of Bob Presto's club.
    - Milton dies on the bridge between the United States and Canada.
    - Water washes away all sins, especially in the act of baptism. Cal is baptized twice: once by Father Mike (she returns the favor at the time) and once in Bob Presto's pool.
    - Cal must look to the future and leave the past as water under the bridge.
- The car-chase scene between Milton and Father Mike figuratively bridges all the gaps in the novel. Symbolically, it stands for all things that are joined together.
- This terrific scene (p.505-511) plays out visually. We can just see the movie:

    > *Father Mike looked up to see Milton's avenging eyes filling the rearview mirror. Milton, gazing ahead into the Gremlin's interior, saw a slice of Father Mike's face.* (p.508)

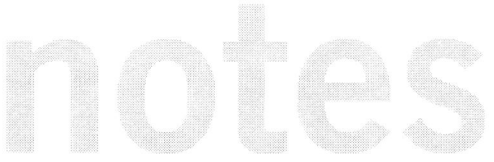

The scene reflects the difference between the reality of life vs. the dream of life. We want to believe that Milton's last thoughts were of his "air-ride" and that he was claimed gently by the waters of time. The reality is that Milton died as a result of his head being crushed against the steering wheel. There is no right way to view life. Like Milton, we will always be astonished by the way it turns out.

- On two occasions Eugenides uses the same water image and the same phrasing to emphasize his point:

    The surface of the sea is a mirror, reflecting divergent evolutionary paths. Up above, the creatures of air; down below, those of water. One planet containing two worlds. (p.297, p.484)

- The first reference is to the girls in Callie's swimming class at school; the second is to the customers in Bob Presto's 69'ers sex club. Different yet the same.
    - In the first scene, the sexual characteristics of the girls (pubic hair, breasts) are proudly shown off by those who have them. Anyone who isn't physically mature, like Cal and other shy, plump girls, try to hide like *"sea lions, lurking in the depths."* (p.297)
    - In Presto's club, viewers look through a peephole at the extraordinary sexual characteristics exhibited by the performers.
- Both groups are curious and fascinated. While the curiosity of the girls is quite acceptable, the curiosity of the customers is not.

Minotaur and the Maze

- The minotaur is the hideous monster of Crete with the head of a man and the body of a bull. He lived in a labyrinth constructed by King Minos and survived by killing the unfortunate captives who were thrown into the maze.

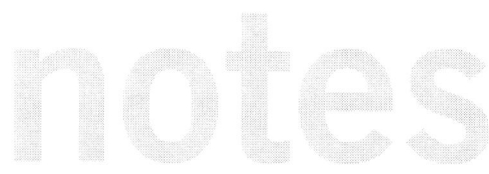

- Milton's Greek connection was his love of the minotaur films and stories to which he exposed the young Callie. This becomes an apt symbol for Cal/Callie because his entire early life is a search for a way out of the maze of confused sexuality. After reading Dr. Luce's report, Callie sees herself as a monster in need of escape.
- To Desdemona, pregnancy is also a maze from which there is no escape:

    > *Desdemona kept turning this way and that, left side, right side, trying to find a comfortable position. Without leaving her bed, she wandered the dark corridors of pregnancy, stumbling over the bones of women who had passed this way before her.* (p.113)

- Lefty and Desdemona are hunted by a minotaur of their own making. Desdemona, especially, fears the revelation of their secret crime.

Gambling

- As good a writer as Eugenides is, he still enjoys using common symbolism – gambling – to represent the role of fate and destiny. Lefty is a gambler in his youth, and he gambles when he lets Jimmy take him into a life of crime. Much later, he ends up literally betting away the family's fortune.
- This gambling metaphor highlights the genetic crapshoot that eventually begets Cal.

Numbers

- **Four.** The novel is divided into four sections; there are four parts to Jung's notion of consciousness: the number four encompasses the complete cycle of life – birth, childhood, adulthood, and death. These are all processes of transformation.

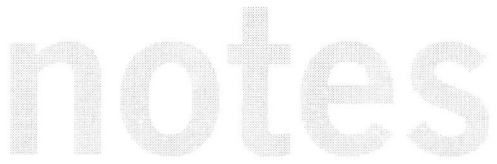

- **Eleven.** Cal has a brother named Chapter 11; there is an eleven-year gap in the story (p.168); eleven is "the devil's dozen" – a negative number.

    If we continue to play the numbers game, eleven sits between ten and twelve. The number ten represents completion and perfection (ten commandments, ten fingers).

- **Twelve** is an equally important number: the twelve months of the cyclical year, the twelve signs of the zodiac, the twelve tribes of Israel, the twelve apostles, the twelve gods in the Greek lineup; all an even dozen.

    Because eleven is in between the perfection of ten and the importance of twelve, it is a number that is off balance, like Cal, in terms of social and cultural recognition.

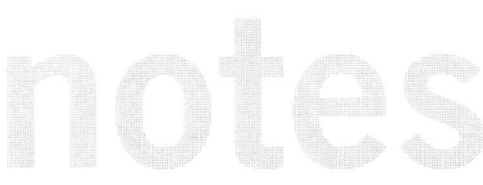

BACKGROUND INFORMATION

Hermaphrodism

The Myth of Tiresius

W.D. Fard

Grandpa's Song

Carl Jung

BACKGROUND INFORMATION

Hermaphrodism

- The accepted definition of hermaphrodite is that of a person born with both male and female sex organs. This is a rare condition, the causes of which are unknown. There are three types of hermaphrodism:
    - The true hermaphrodite has tissue that comes from both the ovaries and the testes. These people are raised in the sex they most resemble.
    - The female pseudohermaphrodite is born with normal female internal organs but has genitals that appear more male than female. This person has an overabundance of testosterone.

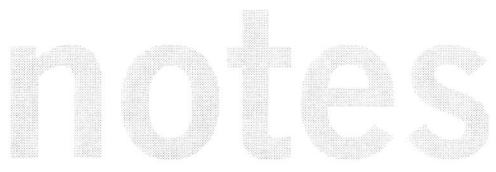

- o The male pseudohermaphrodite is born with an XY chromosome, which indicates a female, but the testes are located elsewhere. The female genital area can be ambiguous-looking. This syndrome (Cal's) is caused by Androgen Insensitivity Syndrome (AIS).

    Zora also has this deficiency but is more physically female in appearance than Cal was. Zora does not want to be either male or female; she is interested only in being what she is – a hermaphrodite. (p.487)

- Androgenital syndrome, known also as 5-alpha-reductase deficiency syndrome, is difficult to assess. Some cultures assign these children to a separate group for early child rearing in one sex or the other (nurture). The most common "switch" to male identity occurs at puberty and is completed surgically.
- The Intersex Society of North America (ISNA) is an organization devoted to making changes to end the shame, the secrecy, and the unwanted genital surgeries for people like Cal. This novel is devoted to the same goal.

The Story of Mythological Tiresias

Argument between Zeus & Hera

- One day while walking on Mount Cyllene, Tiresias (whose name means "interpreter of signs") saw two serpents coupling. On striking one of them, he was transformed into a woman. He, now she, lived as a woman for seven years until, by the same method, she was changed back to a man. Some say that Tiresias changed back and forth like this six times and finally ended his life as a crone.

- Other versions of the story say that Tiresias was once called upon to settle an argument between Zeus and Hera over whether males or females experienced the greatest pleasure when making love. After being involved in a ménage à trois with them, he declared that the woman experienced greater pleasure. Hera was angry at this (though why is unclear) and blinded him. Zeus, to compensate, gave Tiresias the gift of prophecy.

- When Tiresias was to leave the earth he didn't die but was carried directly to the underworld (Hades), where together with Persephone he serves as mediator between the living and the dead.

- For the ancient Greeks, Tiresias, the character, allegorically represented the seasons. Spring is considered a masculine season and it is in this time that he strikes the serpent and is changed to the feminine gender. The season changes to summer, considered to be feminine, as all plants blossom in that season. As summer draws to a close and autumn approaches, Tiresias returns to being a male. At the end of this time, he judges the argument between Zeus and Hera and is once again transformed into a woman. In the spring, Zeus gives him second sight; he transforms back into a man and the cycle begins anew.

W. D. Fard

- The real W. D. Fard (c.1891 – c.1934) was the founder of the Temple of Islam, an American Black Muslim religious movement that later became known as the Nation of Islam. This W.D. Fard had a number of aliases:

Wali Fard, Wali Fard Muhammad, Farad Muhammad, Master Farad Muhammad, Wallace D. Fard, Wallace Fard Muhammad, W. D. Farad, W. D. Farrad, Wali Farad, Wallace Delaney Fard, Wallace Dodd Fard, F. Mohammed Ali.

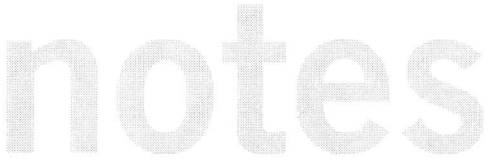

- What is known of this W.D. Fard is that in the summer of 1930 he sold dry goods door to door in the area of Detroit. Suddenly, on the fourth of July, he made a speech announcing the establishment of the Temple of Islam. A second temple was later formed in Chicago in 1932 by one of his disciples. In 1933, Fard moved to Chicago and disappeared shortly afterward.

- His origins are mysterious. He has been identified as having mixed ethnic heritage, and he might have come from any one of the following places: New Zealand, Oregon, India, Arabia, Britain, West Indies, or California.

- His speeches were dedicated to black separatist issues and to empowering blacks to fight for their independence, self-confidence, and rights. He did this from a platform that emphasized Islam as the proper foundation for these struggles. All disciples were encouraged to become Muslim.

- His theories were not traditionally Muslim but were based on the fictional story that a mad black scientist named Yakub created white people six thousand years ago as a curse and test for the superior black people. Fard himself claimed to be sent by Allah to reclaim his downtrodden people.

- In the last years following the Depression, Detroit was not a calm place to be. There was racial tension and a case of ritual killing for which a member of the Nation of Islam was arrested for the "sacrifice" of a man. Fard was arrested in this incident but was let go. Soon after he disappeared again.

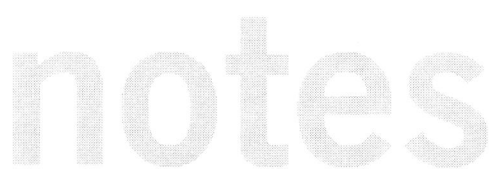

Grandpa's Song

Written by Dwight Latham & Moe Jaffe, 1947

Many many years ago, when I was twenty-three,
I was married to a widow as pretty as can be,
This widow had a grown-up daughter who had hair of red,
My father fell in love with her and soon the two were wed.
This made my dad my son-in-law and changed my very life,
For my daughter was my mother, for she was my father's wife.
To complicate the matter, even though it brought me joy,
I soon became the father of a bouncing baby boy.
My little baby thus became a brother-in-law to dad,
And so became my uncle, though it made me very sad,
For if he was my uncle then that also made him brother
To the widow's grown-up daughter, who of course was my step-mother.
Father's wife then had a son who kept them on the run.
And he became my grandchild for he was my daughter's son.
My wife is now my mother's mother and it makes me blue,
Because although she is my wife, she's my grandmother, too.
Oh, if my wife's my grandmother then I am her grandchild.
And every time I think of it, it nearly drives me wild.
For now I have become the strangest case you ever saw –
As the husband of my grandmother, I am my own grandpa.

Chorus:
I'm my own grandpa, I'm my own grandpa.
It sounds funny, I know, but it really is so –
I'm my own grandpa.

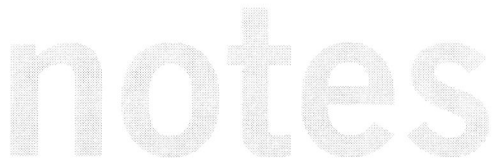

Carl Jung

- Jung (1875-1961) was a Swiss psychiatrist and psychologist, who formed his revolutionary psychological theories under the influence of such philosophers as Kant, Goethe, Schopenhauer, and Nietzsche.

- He is most famous for his theory of the collective unconscious and for the ideas of animus and anima – the duality of the human subconscious ego.

- The collective unconscious encompasses the spirit of the world's history and knowledge. It is the bank that holds man's ancestral experiences, which can surface in the consciousness of an individual at anytime and anywhere.

- The theories identifying animus and anima relate to the union of opposites, i.e., the combination of male and female characteristics embedded in an individual ego. A man's subconscious will balance itself with female qualities; a woman's subconscious will do the same with male qualities. How much depends on each individual.

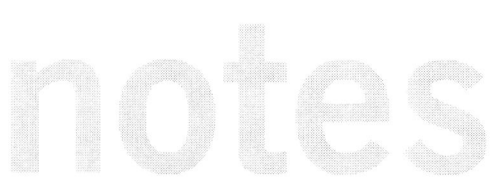

FROM THE NOVEL...
Quotes

FROM THE NOVEL...

Memorable Quotes from the text of Middlesex

PAGE 3. I was born twice: first, as a baby girl, on a remarkably smogless Detroit day in January of 1960; and then again, as a teenage boy, in an emergency room near Petoskey, Michigan, in August of 1974. Specialized readers may have come across me in Dr. Peter Luce's study, "Gender Identity in 5-Alpha-Reductase Pseudohermaphrodites," published in the Journal of Pediatric Endocrinology in 1975. Or maybe you've seen my photograph in chapter 16 of the now sadly outdated Genetics and Heredity. That's me on page 578, standing naked beside a height chart with a black box covering my eyes.

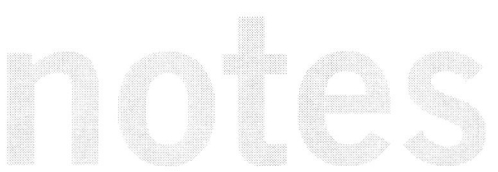

PAGE 9. Of course, a narrator in my position (prefetal at the time) can't be entirely sure about any of this. I can only explain the scientific mania that overtook my father during that spring of '59 as a symptom of the belief in progress that was infecting everyone back then. Remember, Sputnik had been launched only two years earlier. Polio, which had kept my parents quarantined indoors during the summer of their childhood, had been conquered by the Salk vaccine. People had no idea that viruses were cleverer than human beings, and thought they'd soon be a thing of the past. In that optimistic, postwar America, which I caught the tail end of, everybody was the master of his own destiny, so it only followed that my father would try to be the master of his.

PAGE 39. Joking but not joking, Desdemona and Lefty embraced. At first they just hugged in the standard way, but after ten seconds the hug began to change; certain positions of the hands and strokings of the fingers weren't the usual displays of sibling affection, and these things constituted a language of their own, announced a whole new message in the silent room.

PAGE 106. Like most hermaphrodites but by no means all, I can't have children. That's one of the reasons why I've never married. It's one of the reasons, aside from shame, why I decided to join the Foreign Service. I've never wanted to stay in one place. After I started living as a male, my mother and I moved away from Michigan and I've been moving ever since.

PAGE 252. Shameful as it is to say, the riots were the best thing that ever happened to us. Overnight we went from being a family desperately trying to stay in the middle class to one with hopes of sneaking into the upper, or at least the upper-middle.

PAGE 285, 286. As Miss Grotowski sketches equations on the board, my classmates all around me begin to change....Only Calliope, in the second row, is motionless, her desk stalled somehow, so that she's the only one who takes in the true extent of the metamorphoses around her...and Calliope feels gypped, cheated. "Remember me?" she says, to nature. "I'm waiting. I'm still here."

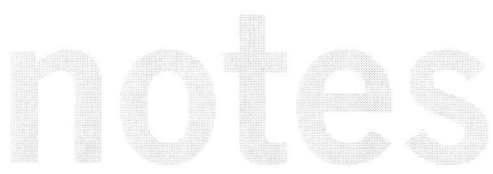

PAGE 401. From my birth, when they went undetected, to my baptism where they upstaged the priest, to my troubled adolescence when they didn't do much of anything and then did everything at once, my genitals have been the most significant thing that ever happened to me.

PAGE 408. He was trying to act casual [Dr. Luce], but I could see he was excited. I was an extraordinary case, after all. He was taking his time, savoring me. To a scientist like Luce I was nothing less than a sexual or genetic Kaspar Hauser.

PAGE 413. In other words, before even seeing me, Luce was able to make an educated guess that I was a male pseudohermaphrodite – genetically male but appearing otherwise, with 5-alpha-reductase deficiency syndrome. But that, according to Luce's thinking, did not mean that I had a male gender identity.

My being a teenager complicated things. In addition to chromosomal and hormonal factors, Luce had to consider my sex of rearing, which had been female.

PAGE 418. Half the time I wrote like bad George Eliot, the other half like bad Salinger. "If there's one thing I hate it's television." Not true: I loved television! But on that Smith Corona I quickly discovered that telling the truth wasn't nearly as much fun as making things up. I also knew that I was writing for an audience – Dr. Luce – and that if I seemed normal enough, he might send me back home. This explains the passages about my love of cats ("feline affection"), the pie recipes, and my deep feelings for nature.

PAGE 445. I opened my eyes. And in the mirror I didn't see myself. Not the Mona Lisa with the enigmatic smile any longer. Not the shy girl with the tangled black hair in her face, but instead her fraternal twin brother. With the screen of my hair removed, the recent changes in my face were far more evident. My jaw looked squarer, broader, my neck thicker, with a bulge of Adam's apple in the center. It was unquestionably a male face, but the feelings inside that boy were still a girl's. To cut off your hair after a breakup was a feminine reaction. It was a way to start over, to renounce vanity, to spite love. I knew that I would never see the Object again. Despite bigger problems, greater worries, it was heartbreak that seized me when I first saw my male face in the mirror. I thought: it's over. By cutting off my hair I was punishing myself for loving someone so much. I was trying to be stronger.

PAGE 446. I had miscalculated with Luce. I thought that after talking to me he would decide that I was normal and leave me alone. But I was beginning to understand something about normality. Normality wasn't normal. It couldn't be. If normality were normal, everybody could leave it alone. They could sit back and let normality manifest itself. But people – especially doctors – had doubts about normality. They weren't sure normality was up to the job. And so they felt inclined to give it a boost.

PAGE 446. The tank itself was not that large ... We climbed down a ladder into the warm water. From the booths, you looked directly into the tank; it was impossible to see above the surface. So we could keep our heads out of the water, if we wanted, and talk to one another while we worked. As long as we submerged ourselves from the waist down the customers were content. "They didn't come here to see your pretty face," was how Presto put it to me. All this made it much easier. I don't think I could have performed in a regular peep show, face-to-face with the voyeurs. Their gaze would have sucked my soul out of me.

PAGE 489. I wasn't the only one! Listening to Zora, that was mainly what hit home with me. I knew right then that I had to stay in San Francisco for a while. Fate or luck had brought me here and I had to take from it what I needed. It didn't matter what I might be compelled to do to make money. I just wanted to stay with Zora, to learn from her, and to be less alone in the world. I was already stepping through the charmed door of those druggy, celebratory, youthful days. By that first afternoon the soreness in my ribs was already lessening. Even the air seemed on fire, subtly aflame with energy as it does when you are young, when the synapses are firing wildly and death is far away.

PAGE 495. I was more interested in historical than medical material ... I became acquainted with the hijras of India, the kwoluaatmwols of the Sambia in Papua New Guinea, and the guevedoche of the Dominican Republic. Karl Heinrich Ulrichs, writing in Germany in 1860, spoke of das dritte Geschlecht, the third gender. He called himself a Uranist and believed that he had a female soul in a male body. Many cultures on earth operated not with two genders but with three. And the third was always special, exalted, endowed with mystical gifts.

PAGE 519, 520. Tessie Stephanides, who in a different lifetime when space travel was new had decided to go along with her husband and create a girl by devious means, now saw before her, in the snowy driveway, the fruit of that scheme. Not a daughter at all anymore but, at least by looks, a son. She was tired and heartsick and had no energy to deal with this new event. It was not acceptable that I was not living as a male person. Tessie didn't think it should be up to me ... [Still] Tessie was going to try to accept things. She felt crushed by what had happened to me but she was going to endure it for my sake.

ACKNOWLEDGEMENTS

ACKNOWLEDGEMENTS

Collins, Rachel. "Through Gendered Eyes: Jeffrey Eugenides' Middlesex." *Library Journal.* July 2002.

Elliot, T. S. "The Fire Sermon." *The Waste Land and Other Poems.* Great Britain: Faber and Faber, 1940.

"Jeffrey Eugenides." *Authors & Artists for Young Adults.* Vol. 51. Farmington Hills, MI: Thomson Gale, 2003.

"The Herculine Effort That Grew." *Sydney Morning Herald* (on-line), Oct. 19, 2002. <http://www.smh.com.au>.

Miller, Laura. "Sex, Fate & Zeus, and Hera's Kinkiest Argument." *Salon Books.* <http://www.salon.com>.

"Sexual Differentiation Disorders." *Hermaphrodite Education and Listening Post.* December, 2003.